# The Herd Boy

*For the Mdingi family*
*From Niki Daly*

First published by Jacana Media (Pty) Ltd
First and second impression 2012
Third impression 2013
Fourth impression 2014

10 Orange Street
Sunnyside
Auckland Park 2092
South Africa
+2711 628 3200
www.jacana.co.za

ISBN 978-1-4314-0102-4

Set in 15 on 21pt Cantoria MT
Title lettering and text layout by Sally Swart
Printed and bound by Craft Print International Ltd
Job no. 002188

See a complete list of Jacana titles at www.jacana.co.za

*Generously supported by Tata Steel*

*The author wishes to thank Basil Mills of the*
*National English Literary Museum for his guidance*
*on cultural details.*

# The Herd Boy

Written and illustrated by Niki Daly

JACANA

"*Vuka!* Wake up, Malusi!" Mama calls.

Inside, the hut is still dark. Outside, the air is cool and the sun is rising – first a red rim along the surrounding hills, then turning to gold as it rises and starts warming the village.

*Mielie pap* is steaming in the pot. "Eat up!" says Mama. "A boy cannot work on an empty stomach."

Malusi looks after his grandfather's sheep and goats.

It's a big job for a small boy.

"*Pweew! Pweew!*" Malusi's shrill whistling drives the sheep out of Grandfather's *kraal*.

By the time they reach the grazing slopes, the earth is hot beneath his bare feet.

Malusi shields his eyes against the sun's glare and looks up. There, high in the sky, flying in wide circles, he spots a Black Eagle.

He places his feet carefully as he moves through the bush where puff adders doze, coiled up and unseen.

He keeps the sheep and goats from straying towards the deep *donga*, which is easy to fall into, but hard to climb out of.

You have to be awake, and you have to be brave to be a herd boy.

Along the *krans*, a troop of baboons gather. If they come down, he will use his voice and a handful of stones to drive them back.

"Woof!" He hears Koko barking.

That means his friend, Lungisa, is only a shout away.

Lungisa is older than Malusi and has his own dog.

Sometimes they meet and play games while the sheep graze. Lungisa always wants to play two-man football and stick-fight. Malusi likes a challenge. Koko jumps out of their way as they kick up the dust.

"*Shu!*" yells Malusi, in the middle of the fight, "I'm hot!" So they break while he removes his blanket… slowly… giving him time to plan how to win a few points. But he never does.

Lungisa is the champion footballer *and* champion stick-fighter. Still, Malusi is a quick learner. He knows he must keep his eye on the ball and move out of harm's way during a stick-fight.

It's lunchtime and Zolika, his older sister, brings their lunch.

Every day, it is the same thing – *umvubo*, a sour mixture of curdled milk and *mielie pap*. He and Lungisa always eat it all up and scrape the tin bowls with their fingers.

"When I grow up," says Lungisa, "I'm going to play football for Bafana Bafana."

"When I grow up," says Malusi quietly, "I'm going to be President."

Lungisa laughs so loudly that it sets the baboons off.

"*Waahoo! Waahoo!*" they holler back. Zolika collects the bowls. "Malusi is clever," she says. "He can be anything he likes."

Malusi is glad when Lungisa disappears into the dip to join his flock.

Malusi likes being on his own – just him and his shadow. Dead quiet and as still as a mountain, he watches the ground, where two columns of termites are on the march. *Eish*! Such hard workers – all working together.

If he sees one on its own, he feels sorry for it, and says, "*Hamba*! Go away, little *gogga*. Go and join your people."

*Push-push, roll-roll,*
*push-push, roll-roll.*
Malusi smiles at the dung beetle
who never gives up. It rests in Malusi's
shadow and then pushes on into the
harsh sunlight.

It reminds Malusi what he must still
do – collect some fresh dung to give to
the shopkeeper, uMdinga, who will add
it to the soil in his garden. In return,
Malusi's mother will receive some
fresh vegetables.

He practises his counting as he
scoops up the dung pebbles:
*nye* – one... *mbini* – two...
*ntathu* – three... until the sack is filled.

*Haai wena!* When he looks up, there's an old baboon sitting on a rock – and it is much too close to the baby lambs and kids.

Malusi shakes his stick and shouts, "*Hamba!*"

The baboon is thin and looks hungry. When he opens his jaws, he is missing one fang. Still, Malusi does not like the look of him, and when he suddenly climbs off the rock and moves forward, it is time to shout much louder.

"*Lungisaaaaa! Kokooooo!*"

His voice echoes off the *krans*.

Now the bush is filled with Malusi's cries and the bleating of the frightened herd.

The baboon is among the sheep and goats! If he does not take a young one, he will scare the animals towards the *donga*. Malusi moves cautiously among the flock – stick at the ready.

Then he spots the baboon's tail, hears the cry of a lamb and sees the dust of a struggle.

"*Maluuuusi!*"

It's Lungisa coming with Koko. Koko smells the baboon and dashes in between the frightened animals – who clear a ring for the fight. Lungisa and Malusi push themselves forwards, ready to help Koko.

But there is no fight.

Koko's blood-curdling growls and bared teeth have changed the baboon's mind. He lets go of the bleeding lamb and scuttles back up the slope.

The lamb is injured, but still alive. Maybe, grandfather can put some medicine on its wounds and make it better.

For now, Malusi wraps his blanket around the little lamb and pats Koko.

"I wish I had a dog like you," he says to the panting dog.

"He's like Baby Jake," brags Lungisa. Malusi has to agree. Koko is short but very powerful, like the famous boxer – Baby Jake Matlala.

The heat has gone out of the day, and it is time to go home. Lungiso offers to carry uMdingi's dung so that Malusi can carry the injured lamb. Koko barks at the herd, driving them down the slope towards the dirt road that leads to the kraal.

*"Yes, mother, we are hungry!*
*Is the fire burning?*
*Is the food cooking?*
*Yes, mother we are returning!"*

Malusi and Lungisa sing this song along the dirt road. Then they stop.

"Look," says Lungisa. "A car is coming!"

Malusi sees it approach in a cloud of dust.

They move the sheep to the side of the road. But the car does not pass. Instead, it slows down and stops.

"Who has such a smart, shiny car?" wonders Malusi.

Slowly, the back window opens and an old man with a face as lined as the *krans* smiles at them.

"*Molweni!*" greets the old man.

"*Molo Tat'omkhulu*," the boys return his greeting.

He tells them that, when he was a young boy, he also wore a red blanket and looked after sheep. Malusi looks at the beautiful shirt he is wearing now and quickly looks down.

"So what do you boys want to be when you grow up?" asks the old man.

"To play for Bafana Bafana," answers Lungisa.

Malusi is too shy to answer, so Lungisa answers for him.

"He wants to be the president," says Lungisa, giggling.

Then the old man sees what Malusi has been carrying and says, "Ah, a boy who looks after his herd will make a very fine leader. *Sala kahle*, Mr President."

The sun has dipped behind the hills, casting long shadows across the *veld*.

The soft padding of hooves on clay makes gentle music. Voices can be heard coming from the kraal.

Malusi hopes his grandfather will not be angry because he has brought home a wounded lamb. Surely he will know that Malusi has done his very best to save it.

Maybe the little lamb will survive.

Before bedtime, a pup is brought to
Malusi.

"uMdingi sent this for you," says his
grandfather. "I'm told that Koko is his dad,
so those baboons had better watch out!"

Malusi smiles and opens his blanket
for the pup to crawl under.

All is well.

In the darkness of the hut, Malusi
repeats the words of the old man:

*"A boy who looks after his herd will
make a fine leader."*

Then he closes his tired eyes and
falls asleep...

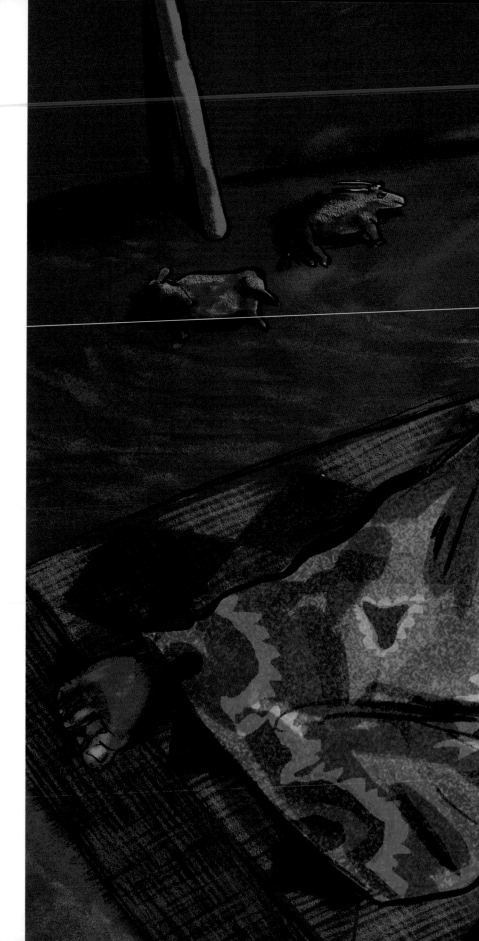

where a dream
is waiting to be dreamed.

VIVA! PRESIDENT MALUSI

VIVA PRE

*A note from the Author:*

Many great men come from humble beginnings. One such was the boy, David, of the Old Testament who looked after his father's flocks and later rose to become a king. Muhammad, too, spent part of his boyhood, in all weathers and amid dangers, tending to his family's herd.

A great and much-loved man of our own time – former president Nelson Rolihlahla Mandela, also came from a humble, rural background. Just who could have predicted that a herd boy from the village of Qunu in the Transkei would, one day, become a great world leader?

Though our childhoods may appear accidental – some luckier than others – they, so often, seem custom made for the adults we become. So I ask, "What is there in the life of a herd boy that would help prepare him to become the shepherd of a nation?"

**Glossary:**

**Bafana** (Xhosa) *bar-far-nah*, boys, (Bafana Bafana is a South African football team)

**Donga** (Anglo-Indian) *dong-gah*, usually dry, washed-out gulley

**Eish!** (Xhosa; slang) *eesh*, exclamation expressing surprise

**Gogga** (Afrikaans) *chaw-cha* ('ch' as in 'loch'), a little insect

**Haai wena!** (Xhosa) *high-where-nah*, exclamation of alarm as in 'oh no!' or 'gosh!'

**Hamba!** (Xhosa) *hum-bah*, go or go away

**Kraal** (Dutch/S African): *kraa-el*, an enclosure for animals near a homestead

**Krans** (from German: *Kranz*) *kraa-ns*, an overhanging cliff-face

**Mielie pap** (Afrikaans) *mee-lee pup*, maize porridge

**Molo Tat'omkhulu** (Xhosa) *maw-lor taa-toom-cool-loo*, hello Grandfather

**Molweni** (Xhosa) *mawl-where-nee*, hello (plural)

**Nye, mbini, ntathu** *(Xhosa)* *'n-yeh, 'm-bee-nee, 'n-taa-too*, numbers one, two and three

**Sala kahle!** (Xhosa) *Sah-lah kah-shlay*, stay well!

**Shu!** (Xhosa) *shoo*, hot

**uMdingi** (Xhosa) *oo-m-dingy*, u is the title Mr, hence Mr Mdingi

**Umvubo** (Xhosa) *oom-voo-boo*, a mixture of curdled sour milk and maize porridge

**Veld** (South African) *felt* wild open country

**Vuka!** (Xhosa) *voo-ka*, wake up!